The Whodunit? Detective Agency

The Café Mystery

GROSSET & DUNLAP
Published by the Penguin Group
Penguin Group (USA) LLC, 375 Hudson Street, New York, New York 10014, USA

USA | Canada | UK | Ireland | Australia | New Zealand | India | South Africa | China

penguin.com
A Penguin Random House Company

Original title: LasseMajas Detektivbyrå: Cafémysteriet
Text by Martin Widmark
Original cover and illustrations by Helena Willis

English language edition copyright © 2015 Penguin Group (USA) LLC. Original edition published by Bonnier Carlsen Bokförlag, Sweden, 2003. Text copyright © 2003 by Martin Widmark. Illustrations copyright © 2003 by Helena Willis. Published in 2015 by Grosset & Dunlap, a division of Penguin Young Readers Group, 345 Hudson Street, New York, New York 10014. GROSSET & DUNLAP is a trademark of Penguin Group (USA) LLC. Manufactured in China.

Library of Congress Cataloging-in-Publication Data is available.

ISBN 978-0-448-48072-5 (pbk)   10 9 8 7 6 5 4 3 2 1
ISBN 978-0-448-48073-2 (hc)   10 9 8 7 6 5 4 3 2 1

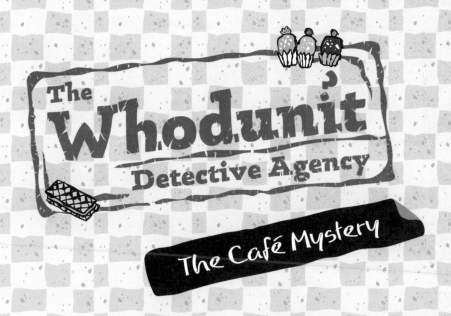

The Whodunit Detective Agency

The Café Mystery

Martin Widmark
illustrated by Helena Willis

Grosset & Dunlap
An Imprint of Penguin Group (USA) LLC

MUSEUM STREET

Museum

PLEASANT VALLEY r SC

News

Church

CHURCH STREET

Post Office

The Jeweler

HOT DOG

The Whodunit Detective
Agency Headquarters

The Café Mystery

The books in *The Whodunit Detective Agency* series are set in the charming little town of Pleasant Valley. It's the kind of close-knit community where nearly everyone knows one another. The town and characters are all fictional, of course . . . or are they?

The main characters, Jerry and Maya, are classmates and close friends who run a small detective agency together.

The people:

Jerry

Maya

Ella
Bernard

Sara
Bernard

Steve
Marzipan

Dino
Panini

CHAPTER 1

Photos and Apple Pie

"**M**mm, pastries!" said Maya.

"Cakes and muffins! Yum," added Jerry.

"Can you believe everything that's been happening in there?" asked Maya, gesturing toward Café Marzipan, Pleasant Valley's best bakery. "It's hard to imagine anything *bad* happening when you see all the *good* things in the window. Let's get something to eat and see what we can find out."

"Wait a second," said Jerry. "Let's take a photo first."

Jerry and Maya now had a new digital camera for their detective agency, and Jerry was taking photos of everything, everyone, and every pastry they saw. You never knew where an important clue might come from!

He took a step back and pointed the camera. Maya leaped in front of the shop window so that she could be in the picture, too.

"You always want to be in the photos!" Jerry laughed. "You'd make an excellent model, but I want to get a picture of the pastries." Jerry took a couple of pictures, even though Maya kept jumping in with a fancy pose.

Then they went into the bakery, which was on Church Street, next to Mohammed Carat's jewelry shop.

Jerry ordered a muffin, and Maya chose a cupcake. The young woman at the cash register was surprisingly quiet and seemed upset about something. It looked like she had been crying.

The two young detectives paid for their treats and looked around the bakery for a place to sit.

"Hello there, my little helpers," they heard someone call. "Come over here and sit with me."

They saw Pleasant Valley's police chief waving at them. The two classmates walked over to the police chief's table and sat down.

"You've just walked into a crime scene, you know," said the police chief, his mouth full of cake. Not one to miss an opportunity, Jerry reached for the camera. Maya realized what Jerry had in mind, and after glaring at him, wiped the frosting off the police chief's nose.

"Thank you," said the police chief and continued with his story: "The robber was here just an hour ago."

"What? Again?" gasped Jerry. He and Maya had read in the local paper that Café Marzipan had already been robbed twice this year.

"So *that's* why the woman at the cash register was upset," said Maya.

"Yes, Sara Bernard is still in shock. Poor thing, she's the one who faced down the robber and had to empty the cash register for the crook," replied the police chief.

"Did the robber take a lot of money?" asked Jerry.

"Yes, that's what's so strange. On all three occasions, there's been an unusual amount of cash here in the café. The first time, the café had extra cash on hand to buy a new coffee

machine. The second time, the rent was due.
Just before the latest incident yesterday,
a busload of soccer players stopped in after
a game. The bakery sold out of all the cakes,
muffins, and pastries, and that's why there
was so much cash in the register.

"That means the robber has gotten away
with loads of money all three times."

"Very strange," agreed Jerry.

"That's a lucky coincidence. Do you
think the robber knows when there's a lot
of money in the register?" asked Maya.

"Excellent question, my clever detective. I'm beginning to think that someone gives him information—someone must tell the robber when he should raid Café Marzipan!"

"He?" asked Maya. "Are we sure that the robber is a man?"

"Another excellent question!" replied the police chief. "We shouldn't jump to conclusions, of course. The tall height Sara reported leads me to believe the robber is a man, but we won't be absolutely certain until we have caught the crook!"

"So, we either have a robber on a lucky streak, or a robber with a connection to the café," Jerry said.

The police chief said nothing for a long moment. He was too busy licking frosting from his face! When he was finished, he said, "The chances of the robber being that lucky three times in a row are low. Just think: He knows exactly when he should strike. Someone must be giving him the information he needs. Does the Whodunit Detective Agency have any ideas on who it might be?"

Jerry lowered his voice to a whisper: "My guess is that it is someone who works here."

"Why do you think that?" asked Maya quietly.

"Someone outside the café might know that they were planning to buy a coffee machine, of course," answered Jerry. "And the same person might also know when it's time to pay the rent. But no one outside of this shop could have predicted, first of all, that a whole soccer team was going to stop by yesterday, and second, how hungry they would be."

The police chief nodded in agreement, and Maya smiled. She realized that their little detective agency had just found a new case.

CHAPTER 2

The Police Chief Blushes

"At first," said the police chief, "I thought that somebody from the staff had *called* the robber. That is the most obvious explanation. But none of the employees saw any of the others use the phone earlier." The police chief paused. "Before you came, I questioned all three of them individually. I thought they wouldn't have much to say, but it was actually the other way around. Each one talked and talked, on and on, probably so that I wouldn't think that she or he was the suspect. I learned a lot about the people who work here."

"Did anybody from the staff leave the bakery this morning?" asked Maya.

The police chief smiled, guessing Maya's theory.

"You mean the old Superman trick?" he said and laughed. "Somebody who pretends to step out to buy the paper, but then returns in disguise. No, nobody left the premises."

Maya and Jerry looked around Café Marzipan. Somebody in here was in cahoots with a robber!

The woman by the display window said hello to the young detectives.

"That's Ella Bernard. She's a fantastic pastry chef!" said the police chief. "She bakes all the delicious things you see here. I just learned that Ella wants to move to a bigger town and open her own bakery. For that you need money, and a lot of it."

"Bernard? That's the same last name as the woman at the cash register," said Maya.

"That's right. Ella is Sara's mother," explained the police chief.

Jerry and Maya looked at Ella, who was rearranging things in the display window.

She was putting out fresh cakes and pastries. She worked with quick, decisive movements. She clearly knew exactly how she wanted things to look.

When she finished, she turned toward Sara.

"Shh, stop crying," she whispered to her daughter, who was sniffling behind the counter.

"You won't make things any better by crying into the coffee," she continued. "Try to calm down before Steve gets here."

Maya and Jerry could tell that both the mother and daughter were on edge. Maybe it was the stress of the recent robberies. However, Ella cheered up when she mentioned Steve.

"Who's Steve?" asked Maya.

"Steve Marzipan owns the bakery," explained the police chief. "You may have seen him around town. He usually wears thick glasses."

"It sounds like Ella likes him," said Maya.

"That may be so. He's a lucky guy, in that case," sighed the police chief as he looked at Ella, who had taken a little mirror and a lipstick from the pocket in her apron.

When Ella saw that the police chief was looking at her, she smiled, which made the police chief blush and look away.

"Maybe it's the owner, Steve Marzipan, who provides the robber with information," suggested Jerry.

"I doubt it's him," replied the police chief. "Steve's hardly ever here. Ella's the one who takes care of nearly everything in the bakery."

"I'm sorry this took so long," they heard someone behind them say. "But this has been a strange morning, as you may have heard. Your caffe latte, sir."

A tall, thin

man leaned forward and placed a pale brown, steaming-hot drink in front of the police chief.

"Caffe latte?" said Maya wonderingly.

"An espresso—that's strong coffee— mixed with hot milk," explained the tall man, before heading back to the coffee machine again.

"That's Dino Panini," the police chief told her. "Dino makes the best coffee in Pleasant Valley. He's from Italy, and he really knows his beans. But if you remind him of his home country, he gets upset. Apparently, his mother is ill and needs expensive hospital care. 'Mamma mia!

Always money,' he moaned when I questioned him earlier today."

"It sounds like the only person in here who *doesn't* need money is Sara Bernard, the woman at the cash register," observed Jerry.

"Actually, she's not above suspicion, either," replied the police chief. "Sara told me that she's fed up with her mother's bossy attitude and wants to move out. Getting an apartment and buying new furniture doesn't come cheap."

"That means that all the people working here have a reason for wanting to join forces with the robber," Maya summed up.

"Absolutely right," replied

the police chief. "All three are in great need of money."

"So, we're actually looking for *two* criminals," said Jerry. "One who provides the information from the café, and then the robber himself."

"What do we knew about the robber, other than his height?" asked Maya.

"Sara is probably the best one to answer that," replied the police chief. And with that, he waved to the young woman who was still standing by the cash register, sniffling.

CHAPTER 3

Winking and Waving

Sara left her place by the cash register and came over to the table where Jerry, Maya, and the police chief were sitting.

"Please sit down," said the police chief, offering her a handkerchief. Sara took it and dried her tears. "Could you tell us once more what you know about the robber?" asked the police chief.

Sara sighed deeply. The two friends could tell that she was not eager to talk about the man who had robbed her.

"Well, like I said before," Sara began. "He had a balaclava over his head."

"That means a tight-fitting mask with two holes in it," explained the police chief. "It covers your entire face; to see you have to peep through the holes."

Maya nodded. Both she and Jerry knew perfectly well what a balaclava was.

"He was dressed completely in black," continued Sara. "He came up to the counter and handed me a bag for the money. He was waving around a club in the other hand. I didn't know what to do; Dino nodded at me, so I crammed all the cash we had into the robber's bag. Then he ran out of the café and disappeared as quickly as he had come."

"Dino thought you should give the robber the money?" asked Jerry.

"You should never try to play the hero in this sort of situation," said the police chief seriously.

"Did the man say anything during the robbery?" wondered Maya aloud.

"Not a word the whole time," Sara replied. "He just waved the club around and gave me the bag for the money."

"Think carefully now," said Jerry. "This is very important: Did he do anything strange? Did he do anything that surprised you?"

"Nooo . . . ," replied Sara, shaking her head.

"Did he walk oddly?" asked Maya, nudging Sara to remember any details. "Did he have any unusual labels on his clothes, or did you notice anything else in particular about him?"

"No, not as far as I can remember," said Sara. "I just remember the club, the bag, and the mask. But, wait a minute . . ."

Jerry, Maya, and the police chief leaned closer to Sara, and in turn, Dino and Ella looked curiously at their table.

Sara lowered her voice to a whisper:

"I thought it looked like he was winking at Dino. When I was going to empty the cash drawer, I thought for a moment that the whole thing was just an awful nightmare. Then I looked up, and the robber was still there in front of me—but he wasn't looking at me. He was looking at Dino over by the coffee machine!"

"Aha!" said the police chief. "That's something to go on! Thank you for your help. You can go back to what you were doing."

Maya, Jerry, and the police chief got up to leave the café, and Sara and Ella Bernard and Dino Panini watched them anxiously as they walked toward the door.

"Thank you for the fantastic cake," the police chief said happily to Ella Bernard before they stepped out onto the street.

As they were leaving, a man brushed by them in a hurry.

"Excuse me," he said as he squeezed past the police chief. The police chief stepped aside and said to Jerry and Maya:

"That's Steve Marzipan."

"Hmmm, not wearing any glasses today," Maya observed.

"Could I have . . . ?" said Jerry to the police chief, as he pointed to his camera.

The police chief beamed and immediately posed outside the door to Café Marzipan. As quick as a flash, Maya sneaked up and stood next to him.

Jerry laughed at Maya and took a photo. Afterward, they stood for a moment looking into the display window of the café. Ella had just put out fresh pastries. The display looked even more tempting than before!

With that, they said good-bye to the police chief and started walking home to their detective agency, located in Maya's basement.

Jerry wanted to download the photographs to his computer, and Maya wanted to sit and think about what they had learned during their visit to Café Marzipan.

CHAPTER 4

Pastries and Coffee

Maya and Jerry paused on the sidewalk and looked around. Café Marzipan was next to Mohammed Carat's jewelry shop. That was where Vivian Leander worked, selling rings and necklaces. But now she stood on the pavement outside the jeweler's, looking worried.

"Hello there!" said Maya and Jerry. Vivian nodded in reply, but she was distracted. She looked anxiously up and down Church Street.

"Has something happened?" asked Maya.

"It's absolutely awful!" began Vivian. "Through all the years I've worked here, I've been in charge of the coffee break at work. We drink tea and coffee with Mohammed in his office, and it's my job to prepare the drinks and find something tasty to eat. Café Marzipan never lets me down. The display is always so appetizing, and they change it all the time. Who could resist? Mohammed and Danny usually treat themselves to a cinnamon bun each, and I like a cookie."

"Just a cookie?" asked Jerry, astonished.

"Well, as tempting as the cinnamon buns are, I like to watch what I eat. I'll have a small cookie, an apple, and maybe some yogurt."

" JEWE

Jerry and Maya remembered the jewelry shop's former employee who was never without an apple and shared a wink.

"But now I don't dare anymore!" continued Vivian in despair.

"You don't dare what?" asked Maya.

"Go into Café Marzipan," replied Vivian. "I'm not setting foot in there as long as there's a thief on the loose."

Maya and Jerry wondered whether it was the threat of the robber or the thought of not being able to buy cinnamon buns and cookies that worried Vivian most. They said good-bye and continued their walk home.

Back at their detective agency, Maya immediately sat down in one of the comfy armchairs. With paper and pen in hand, she began summing up what they knew about the raid on Café Marzipan. Jerry turned on the computer and connected the camera.

"There have been three robberies at the café," began Maya. "Each time, the robber has chosen exactly the right moment to strike. Each time, there has been plenty of money in the cash register. This is the main reason to believe that the robber knows *when* to strike."

"Mmm," mumbled Jerry in reply.

He wasn't really listening to Maya as he downloaded the pictures of her and the police chief outside Café Marzipan. Jerry zoomed in on the photos and leaned closer to the screen to see all the details better.

Maya continued, "That would mean that someone who worked in the café was giving information to the robber. Someone was telling him when he should go for it. But why would someone in the café help a thief? . . . Hello, Jerry!" insisted Maya. "Why?"

"He or she needs money, of course," replied Jerry. "They must share everything from the cash register. But don't interrupt me now, Maya. There's something strange about these pictures here . . . ," said Jerry.

Maya continued, not worrying about disturbing Jerry:

"Ella Bernard bakes everything in the café and takes care of the display window. She and her daughter seem to argue a lot with each other, maybe because Ella isn't happy with her job anymore. She wants to move away from Pleasant Valley and open her own café in a big city. And she needs money for that. So it could be Ella who's connected to the robber."

"Well, look at that!" Jerry said in surprise, zooming in on the picture he had taken just before he and Maya went into the café.

"Ella's daughter, Sara," continued Maya, "knows exactly how much money there is in the café. She's in charge of the cash register and is fed up with her mother's bossiness. Sara wants to move out, and she needs money to do that. Sara has a good reason for telling the robber when to strike."

"The display window!" said Jerry. "I think I get it now!"

"Then there's Dino Panini, the coffee expert. He needs money for his sick mother in Italy. And it looked like the robber winked at him. Is it Dino who's working with the robber? Why else would the robber wink at him? Of course, maybe it was hot inside the mask and the sweat was running down into his eyes. But how on earth could the robber know just the right

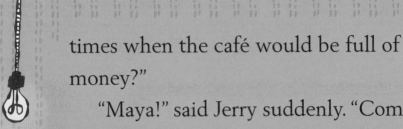

times when the café would be full of money?"

"Maya!" said Jerry suddenly. "Come here and look at this! I think I found the robber's signal! It's like a riddle!"

Jerry pointed to a picture of the display window on his computer screen.

CHAPTER 5

Riddles in the Window

Maya jumped up from her armchair and ran over to Jerry. He was looking at the first picture, which he had taken right before they went into the café.

"Ha-ha!" Maya laughed. "I look like a real model, don't I?"

"But look at the window display!"

"Cakes, muffins, and pastries," said Maya. She wasn't sure why Jerry was so interested in the photo, other than her awesome pose!

"Which types of cakes, muffins, and pastries?" asked Jerry, zooming in on the picture. Maya read the labels in front of the cakes:

"Apple pie, carrot cake, and tea cakes . . ."

She sighed heavily, still not understanding what Jerry was so excited about.

"They're just ordinary pies, cakes, and pastries," she said.

"Look at the first letter of each: *apple* pie, *carrot* cake, and *tea* cakes," said Jerry.

"That makes A, C, and T," said Maya.

"What does that mean? I'm sure it's a riddle."

"What do you mean, a riddle?" asked Maya.

"A word puzzle. You take the first letter of each word and put them together, and then it becomes a message—a message to the robber! What do those letters spell, Maya?"

"A plus C plus T, that makes ACT," said Maya.

"So these aren't just any old cakes," said Jerry eagerly. "Remember Vivian Leander?"

"Vivian Leander! Are you crazy? You don't think she's the robber . . ."

"Don't be silly," replied Jerry. "Remember what Vivian said about the display?"

"Yes," said Maya slowly. "She said they change it frequently." Then, suddenly, she got it.

"Jerry! You're a genius!"

"The message in the window is *act*," said Jerry proudly. "Someone in the café is telling the robber that it is a good time to act . . . to steal from the café! Now look here," he said, switching to the next picture. "Do you remember what they were doing in the café when we were talking to the police chief?"

"Dino was serving coffee, Sara was crying by the cash register, and Ella was arranging the display in the window . . . ," said Maya.

"That's right!" said Jerry, pointing to the computer screen again. "Look at what was in the window when we left Café Marzipan."

Maya leaned closer to the screen and read the labels: "Doughnuts, orange muffins, nutcake, and a tart," Maya said. "D plus O plus N plus T . . . DON'T!"

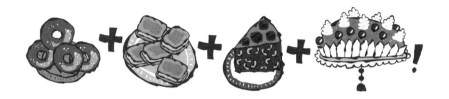

"So that means *Ella* is the one signaling to the robber to tell him when to rob the bakery," said Jerry.

"Come on, Jerry, we need to hurry! We have to go to the police station!"

CHAPTER 6

Act Naturally

"**W**ell, how about that?" said the police chief, impressed with Jerry and Maya's logic. "I think you've discovered something important. This means that if we switch the display in the window, we could lure in the robber."

"That's what we were thinking," said Maya. "And once we've caught him, we can find out why Ella Bernard was helping him."

"This is what we're going to do . . . ," said the police chief to Jerry and Maya.

The three of them sat for a while at the police chief's desk and planned their trap. Finally, everything was ready and they headed over to Café Marzipan.

As they passed Mohammed Carat's jewelry shop, the police chief opened the shop door and called out to Vivian Leander:

"You'll soon be able to wander around town safely again, Miss Leander."

Vivian Leander looked up with surprise, but the police chief, Maya, and Jerry were already on their way to the bakery. Inside Café Marzipan, the police chief asked the employees to gather in the storeroom to talk things over. Jerry and Maya looked around the café.

Once they made sure they were alone, they scrambled to work. They removed the doughnuts, orange muffins, nutcake, and tart from the display, and replaced them with apple pie, carrot cake, and tea cakes instead.

"ACT," read Maya happily. "Now we just need to wait."

Just then, the police chief, Sara, Dino, and

Ella came out of the storeroom. Jerry and Maya nodded secretly to the police chief to let him know everything was ready.

The police chief had told Dino, Sara, and Ella that he had received an anonymous tip: Somebody had called to say that the robber was about to strike again.

"But . . . ," Ella said in surprise, before falling quiet.

The police chief took Sara to one side and whispered to her.

"When should I faint?" they heard Sara ask.

"After you open the cash drawer," whispered the police chief.

Jerry and Maya could see Ella hovering anxiously by the window, but the police chief wasn't going to let her touch anything.

"Everyone, back to your usual positions," he said, clapping his hands. Maya and Jerry each ordered a cinnamon bun and settled in

at a table by the window. Dino went back
to his coffee machine, and Ella fiddled
with cakes and pastries behind the counter.
Sara stood in her normal place behind the
cash register.

Lastly, the police chief crouched down
at Sara's feet, hidden by the register.

"Keep working and act naturally!"
he hissed from his hiding spot. The staff
members continued with their jobs, and
Jerry and Maya enjoyed their buns.

As time passed, Jerry and Maya were
beginning to think that they were mistaken.
Maybe it was just a coincidence that
the cakes were placed that way in the
window.

But now that the trap had been set, they
could only wait and see.

Everyone in the café was looking
nervously from the door to the street.
The robber might come in at any
moment!
        Then the door opened!

CHAPTER 7

A Fainting Cashier

Through the open door walked . . . Roland Sussman! The caretaker who looked after the church in Pleasant Valley! He had a thick scarf around his neck, and his nose was red. Dino, Sara, and Ella relaxed a little. Roland Sussman was sniffing and sneezing.

"Bless you!" said Maya. Roland Sussman noticed the two detectives and smiled, gesturing to his throat.

They understood that he had a sore throat and had lost his voice.

Roland Sussman approached the counter, then stood there for a very long time deciding what to eat.

Finally, he pointed to a brownie and

a cinnamon bun. Ella put the brownie and
the bun in a paper bag and handed it to
Sara at the register. Roland Sussman passed
a bill to Sara, who opened the cash drawer.
Then something unexpected happened!

Sara tripped behind the counter, then quickly recovered her balance—but then she tripped again. What was going on?

It was the police chief tugging at her apron! He thought the robber had come into the café, and he was wondering why Sara wasn't pretending to faint like they'd planned.

Sara managed to stay standing until Roland Sussman had left the bakery, despite the police chief's pulling and tugging.

"What are you doing?" asked Sara, irritated.

"Why didn't you faint like we'd planned?" the police chief snapped in reply.

"That wasn't the—" began Sara, but she didn't finish her sentence, because the door to the café suddenly flew open. And this time there was no doubt—the robber was back!

Like a dangerous wild animal, he had

been lured into a trap without realizing that he would be caught at any moment.

Behind his balaclava mask, his wild eyes quickly looked around the almost-empty bakery. Then he noticed Jerry and Maya by the window! He took a step toward them!

When he saw that they were just children, he put his finger to his lips to tell them to be quiet. He himself didn't say a word.

I wonder why he's so quiet, thought Maya. *Either he has a sore throat like Roland Sussman, or perhaps he doesn't speak English. Most likely he's afraid that his voice will give him away. If he started talking, someone here might recognize his voice.*

The robber went to the register. Ella stood behind the counter, shaking her head subtly. Was she trying to tell the robber something?

But the robber didn't see her. Instead, he looked at Dino Panini, who was standing by the coffee machine with his mouth open.

If Ella is helping the robber, thought Jerry, *why is he looking at Dino?*

By the register, the robber held out the bag for the cash. A terrified Sara pressed the button to open the drawer. Just as it opened, Sara threw up her arms and shrieked. "Aaaaaaaaaah!" She collapsed behind the counter.

The robber wasn't expecting that! What should he do now? He couldn't pick up the money with a club in his hand.

The robber quickly put down the club so he could use both of his hands, then he reached over to stuff the money from the drawer into his bag.

But the police chief's fists shot up from behind the register and grabbed the robber's arms. Suddenly, he was caught in an iron grip! As quick as a flash, the handcuffs were on and the robber couldn't move an inch. The police chief locked the handcuffs to the register. The robber twisted and turned, but he was chained to the spot.

Then the police chief walked around the counter. The robber was about to be unmasked!

CHAPTER 8

Seeing Double

The robber tried to wriggle away, but the police chief grabbed ahold of the mask and pulled it off the robber's head.

And under the balaclava,
it turned out to be . . .

"Steve Marzipan!" said the police chief with surprise.

"What?" said Dino and Sara in unison.

"Are you robbing your own café?" asked Maya.

"You traitor!" hissed Steve Marzipan to Ella Bernard. "The message in the window said that the coast was clear. You lured me into a trap!"

"I promise you, darling," said Ella, beginning to cry. "It wasn't me. It was the children . . ."

"Darling?" the police chief said in disbelief. "Is *that* what this is all about? A love story? Ella arranges the displays in the window for the 'darling' owner Steve, all so that he can come in and frighten the life out of the poor staff here in the café. How selfish!"

The police chief shook his head.

"It's not what you think at all," said Steve.

"I'm not Ella's 'darling.' She just helps me to get tax-free cash out of my own company."

"Tax-free cash?" said the police chief, not understanding.

"Yes, we have to pay taxes on all the money we make," said Steve. "But you don't pay taxes on money that disappears, do you?"

"You've been using me!" shrieked Ella Bernard. "You said we were going to move to a bigger town and that I could open my own café."

"If you don't want to open a new café with my mother, what *do* you want the money for, Steve?" asked Sara pointedly, now furious with both her mother and her boss for putting her through this.

"I want to make a fresh start," replied Steve. "A new life. Yes, I do want to move on, but not to a bigger town, and yes, there is something else I want."

Everyone in the café turned and looked

at one another, trying to understand what Steve was talking about.

Ella was seething with rage.

"What on earth are you talking about?" she yelled. "You lied, you stole, you used me, you scared my daughter, and you tried to frame poor Dino with all your strange winking! The police chief is right—you *are* selfish, Steve!"

"Why would you frame me?" asked Dino Panini. Steve Marzipan's strange behavior clearly came as a shock to him, too.

"What are *you* talking about?" asked Steve. "I never tried to blame the robberies on Dino!"

"But what about all your winking?" asked Jerry.

"Oh, that?" said Steve. "I have terrible eyesight. I hated my old glasses and got these uncomfortable contacts. But my eyes water, and they make me blink and wink all the

time. I need the money to get eye surgery.
I had planned to see the area's best eye
surgeon tomorrow."

"Your new eyes are going to have to wait,"
said the police chief as he fastened Ella
Bernard and Steve Marzipan together with
the handcuffs. "Right now, we're heading for
the police station."

Once the police chief had taken away Ella and Steve, Jerry and Maya were left standing in the café.

"A cup of hot chocolate and a freshly baked muffin, perhaps?" suggested Dino Panini. "We should celebrate now that the case is closed. Let our famous hot chocolate soothe your nerves."

Jerry and Maya felt in their pockets.

"We were in such a hurry, we didn't bring any money with us," said Maya.

"Café *Panini and Bernard* is offering it to you on the house, of course!" said Sara. "As long as Dino and I work here, you can come in anytime and eat for free. We're so grateful that you've helped us out of this terrible situation. It's such a relief now that it's all over."

Maya and Jerry stayed awhile talking to Dino and Sara about everything that had happened.

And the next day, Vivian Leander and everyone else in the town of Pleasant Valley were relieved to read the following article in the paper:

ANOTHER SUCCESS STORY FOR THE WHODUNIT DETECTIVE AGENCY

Pleasant Valley's young detectives, Maya and Jerry, have once again helped the police solve a difficult–but delicious!–case. During their investigation of the Café Marzipan robberies, the Whodunit Detective Agency discovered that the two culprits were the café owner and an employee. The employee/partner in crime used the café's baked goods to send secret messages to the owner/robber. Never before has a seemingly innocent apple pie been used to tell a robber when to steal large sums of money from a cash register.

Jerry and Maya would especially like to thank Vivian Leander, the shop assistant at Mohammed Carat's jewelry shop, who helped with an important clue.

The police chief announced that Steve Marzipan, the culprit and the former owner of the café, will spend his community-service time learning how tax money helps local communities.

Coming soon!

The Whodunit Detective Agency

The Mummy Mystery

A Mysterious Disappearance

The front of the museum was full of reporters and other curious people. Maya and Jerry instantly recognized Barbara Palmer, the museum director, in the middle of the crowd. A few reporters were interviewing her for the news, and Jerry and Maya pushed closer to hear what she had to say.

"No, nothing else has disappeared," she said.

"What does the mummy's note say?" asked a reporter with a microphone.

"I can't tell you that right now," replied the museum director.

Barbara Palmer turned abruptly and walked up the steps toward the museum entrance.

The reporters followed her, and as the

crowd crushed in front of the doorway, Jerry and Maya managed to sneak inside.

"What are you doing in here?" hissed the museum director once she spotted Maya and Jerry. "We are closed today, for obvious reasons. Go away!"

"We can help you find the painting," said Maya firmly.

"Two children? Nonsense! Give me one reason why I should waste my valuable time on you!" snorted Barbara Palmer.

She was pacing to and fro in the museum foyer and cracking her knuckles.

"It's clear the police have nothing to go on, since the museum has already offered a reward of two thousand dollars to anyone who can help find the painting," said Jerry. "You must be desperate."

Barbara Palmer continued nervously walking from one side of the foyer to the other. Maya and Jerry could see that they needed to come up with something to catch the director's attention.

"Have you found the night watchman's cell phone yet?" asked Jerry.

Barbara Palmer stopped and turned. She looked quizzically at the two young detectives.

"How did you know that Mr. Long's phone had disappeared?" she asked.

Jerry smiled. It seemed his lucky guess had brought them one step closer to gaining Barbara Palmer's trust.

"The night watchman had to rush up to your office and call from there. He would have used his cell phone if he had had one."

The museum director was silent for a moment and then said, "Well, all right! I can see that you are keen observers, and the police don't seem to be getting anywhere, anyway. Maybe you can find something they've missed. Follow me!"